C+

KINGDOM PURPOSE

$(a+b)^2$

Tonya Renee

KINGDOM PURPOSE

ISBN 978-1-7371339-5-7

10 9 8 7 6 5 4 3 2 1

Rhema Chariot Publishing

Hello!

Let me explain who I am first and foremost my name is not child, honey, or baby girl. My name is Purpose Shines Jones. That is pronounced SHA-NECE, not shines like the sun, believe me I cannot stand the confusion.

I apologize for sounding rude, harsh, or insensitive. God is still working on me in the rough areas. You see it can be difficult to tell your own story when everyone has their own version they like to distribute from a blind spot. So, I decided to tell it myself.

I live here in a place caught between somewhere and nowhere, we call it the Junction. The name makes it sound like it's a great place to be caught but it is far from a Mayberry experience. We have quite a few businesses in that town that keep it productive and our greatest commodity by far is the high school Osier Elizabeth High.

Because of the Junction's location we have quite a few factories that are stationed on the outskirts of town that have made some in our community flourish a little better than others and they don't mind reminding you about it as well.

The school system has become a melting pot of glue that brings together our town with the other communities surrounding the factories. We are in the middle of everything clustered together but still miles apart. Like I said, the Junction is a rinky-dink town, and I would say my main objective is to get out and never ever look back.

Never! It's nothing to brag about here. I am not a sports fanatic, not hip with the cool kids, I am just me Purpose- oh yea and I prefer to be called Shines (SHA-NECE) got it!

Our town is simply a lot of Mom and Pop stores. We have the Masons it is our rendition of a department store. The Cubbards is the local grocery store and next to them is the pharmacy it is ran by old man Parker and his family. My Mom works in the evening over at Betty's Diner and she goes to school during the day to become a nurse. She drives over an hour to Langston to attend so she can provide generational wealth. She grew up in this area and says it is her generation's responsibility to show us how to endure. I just need her to show me the exit and bus ticket and I will be set. Maybe if she had moved when I was younger, maybe I would look at this differently but at the moment this is what you get.

Anyway!

So, let's talk about me and what drove me to give up on Purpose. Like most people I consider myself you know a Christian. I go to church with my mom on a regular basis. You know it is not like I have a choice, but you know I do love me some God.

Like most people, I get discouraged but most of the time I get comforted when I am in worship. The rest of the time I am just going so I can sit with my BFF Ann, and we can catch up on the latest gossip. Ann's mother works at the local beauty shop, and you know what is spoken in the beauty shop never stays in the beauty shop. Often times some of the major characters are in the midst of the sanctuary commercial free. I consider it two hours of socially charged entertainment. Especially since my life lately is seemingly constantly found in a cycle of uninterrupted issues. Like most I have issues that follow me everywhere I go. That's another reason I love to come and worship.

It allows me the opportunity for a moment in time to cry without being questioned. Pastor Dunlap always says," God collects our tears." Lately it feels like I've been giving God enough to fill a barrel and serve the whole congregation a sip of wine. Isn't it amazing how we can be surrounded by people and they can never recognize the bitter tears of one's soul?

Let the competition begin! Like clockwork Deacon Putts and Mother Watts both have fallen asleep. Is Deacon deep enough sleep to snort and snore or will Mother Watts create a head turner and loose her wig Pastor Dunlap has some serious competition this morning because we got to good breed of horses in the race this morning. *Pastor Dunlap makes his way to the pulpit podium and glares so slightly at the spiritual thoroughbreds.*

Good morning, believers, I just wanted to come to you this morning and leave you with a word of encouragement. Just know whatever you are facing it will not always be like this. Sometimes we

can be in the middle of the storm
for so long, it seems like our vision
is lost and our hearing is muffled
by the attacks of the enemy. We
must not forget that God never
leaves us and we are not forsaken.
God does not need our permission
to send help. He will send angels
to tend to our needs. Let me
validate my statement so you can
place it in the file in your heart
labeled, "Remember me, Lord."
Hebrews 13:2 says, "Do not neglect
to show hospitality to strangers, for
by this some have entertained

angels without knowing it." Be careful who approaches you, they may just have a life saving blessing with your name on it. Choir take us out.

The choir jumps up with an up temple song that shocks Deacon Putts and Mother Watts both out of their sleep. We have a winner! Mother Watts wig has hit the floor! I laughed so loud I thought my belly was going to burst. I just knew mom was going to give me the look, but she didn't. I looked at her, she was sitting there with tears streaming from her eyes. I have never seen my mother cry. I found myself looking at my mother and I found myself saying, "Remember me, Lord!"

Here we go again!

"Girl, can you believe that wig hit the floor again? Shines you hear me talking to you." *I found myself just standing there looking at my mother wondering what made her so upset.*

Ann girl, I'm sorry I got distracted. I know it seems like they would have learned by now to tack that bad boy down.

"Right! Shines, ask your mom if you can come over after church and we can hangout. My folks and I are going over to

Sandersville to eat at the new Chinese restaurant that just opened."

I will ask but I already know it's a no. It doesn't hurt to try! *My mother was standing near the church exit speaking to Pastor Dunlap.* Pastor Dunlap I really enjoyed that message today.

"Sister Jones, I know a lot of folks enjoyed today because it was short and sweet." *Both are laughing as she approaches.* "Well hello Shines! Are you doing ok today?" Yes, I'm doing quite well Pastor.

"That's good, very good."

Momma, Ann, and her family are going over to Sandersville to try the new Chinese restaurant and Ann asked if I could go as well.

"I don't know, you know things are tight this week with exams and we need to save any extra money for travel this week, you understand dear."

Yes, I understand. Same story, same topic! *(She mumbles under breath.)*

Pastor Dunlap says, "Listen Shines, if your mother does not mind maybe I can pay for your meal."

"Oh, Pastor you don't have to do that.", Sis. Jones replies.

"Listen to me it would be a huge favor. I am a huge fan of Chinese food and Shines can check it out for me and if it is not good, she actually would be saving me money. That way me and the wife won't waste a whole evening of time and money checking it out.

Can I Momma, please? Ok, you be on your best behavior. I will, thank you Pastor! I will have my report for you Wednesday after bible study. Pastor Dunlap smiles, "Thank you, look forward to it." Thank you again Pastor, you really didn't have to.

"Sister Jones, it was no problem. Chinese food is really my favorite." *Smiles* "See you Wednesday."

Ann, can you believe I can go!

"Girl I was over here praying Lord it's me again." *Both laughs.* "I hope the food is good. Judy and her family went last week she said it was off the chain."

Ann's whole family is musically inclined, so a road trip with them is always entertaining. By the time you realize it, you have arrived at your destination. We are here and I am starving!

Wow! The aroma lingers from inside as soon as the door swings open. The great thing is the majority of the Sunday crowd has already been through, so we have plenty of room. Me and Ann always try to sit alone so we can girl talk about things that we can't in front of our parents. Which works out fine because her twin brothers usually sit in a booth with their parents.

"Did you get enough on those plates Shines?" Ann jokingly says. Girl, you know I love some Chinese food.

Ann continues, "You eat and never gain a pound from it that what gets me."

Yeah, you know an hour later we will be hungry again, *both girls laugh.*

"Shines, have you decided
what you're going to write your
report on for midterm final
assignment. You know it's worth
thirty-five percent of our grade."
I don't know, not yet I've been
thinking about it. Maybe we can go
to the library after school next
weekend, and we can work on
them a bit.
"Girl you the only one I know that
will waste a weekend in a book.
You know I would rather spend
my weekend at the mall window
shopping."

Yeah Right! If you are looking through a window, you are peeping at a boy chick! Ann replies, "YOU BETTER KNOW IT!", both laugh intensely.

Well, well, look at what we have here Becca, I thought I smelled something sour in here. I assumed it was the cabbage but here's the source. (She reaches over flicks Shines' ponytail and laughs.) "Watch yourself Dottie!", Ann replies.

Dottie continues to belittle the two girls. What you got to say

Ann? Ann, Ann in need of a man it's too bad your face flat like a frying pan. "Dottie don't come for me, and I won't come for you!"

I'm always available! Is that an invitation or do I need to set up an appointment for both of you? I'm running a two for one butt whooping on Thursday! Get with my secretary on Monday morning before I get booked up. *Dottie and Becca walk off snickering just as Ann's mother approaches the table.*

"Hi, Mrs. Vivian" Dottie says smiling. Hi, Dottie and Becca, are you here with your parents? "No ma'am, we are here with Becca's grandparents." Oh, ok well tell them I said hello. "We will "as they walk away still snickering Dottie looks at Shines and winks.

Well girls, are you ready to go? Hope you got enough to eat. Was it up to your expectations Shines? I know you are a connoisseur of everything Asian cuisine, you ok dear.

"Oh, yes I'm sorry I'm so full I think I slipped in a mini coma." *Ann's mother laughs*, well we will definitely have to bring you guys again.

Thanks mom, "yes thank you Mrs. Vivian."

As they make there way to the front of the restaurant Shines feels an eerie feeling come over her as if someone is watching her. Ann notices the peculiar look on her friend's face and says, "Girl, you, ok? You're not worried about that Dottie nonsense?"

No, I felt like someone was watching me.

"Girl, they are the waiters making sure we go pay before we leave. *(laughs)*"

You're right, I'm just being silly but in the back of her mind Shines felt like something was happening and she was unable to stop it, almost like a runaway train caboose and no engineer around to catch it in time. Catastrophe seemed to be waiting right around the corner and she was dead smack in its direction.

The ride home seemed longer than the ride to the restaurant. The twins and Ann both had fallen asleep in the back of the car. Mrs. Vivian drove back while Mr. Taylor rested in the passenger seat. I was in the back thinking about the eerie feeling at the restaurant. *Mrs. Vivian is humming, and notices Shines awake in the rearview mirror.* Shines you're not taking a nap? "No ma'am, I try to stay up with mom when we are on the road. I guess I'm used to keeping her alert." Oh, that's sweet of you. *She goes back to humming.*

"Mrs. Vivian, what's that song you are humming?"

Oh dear, it's one of my favorite songs. It got me through a lot of dark nights, "*Nobody but Jesus by Vanessa Bell Armstrong.*"

"It sounds nice. I will have to look it up when I get home."

I love how God will talk to us through many different instruments in some of our darkest hours. *With a puzzled look upon her face Shines whispers, "instruments, darkest hours?"*

You know it's like Pastor spoke about God sending angels to bring us messages and directions. He will also encourage us with a song in our spirit to remind us that He is concerned and is with us in some of the hardest times if we open our heart to him. What did Pastor say this morning? *Shines says it again, "Remember me, Lord" just as they pull up in front of her home.* Well, we are here.

"Thanks again for letting me go." No problem dear, no problem at all. *Ann wakes up to say bye and the girls both say see you in the morning.*

As Shines watches the car drive off in the distance from a crack in the door, she still has a feeling that something is around the corner about to knock on her door. She is about to cross a threshold that will destroy her or save her.

Threshold

Another Monday morning Purpose's mother Elaine is preparing to hit the road and start her day. She first has to make sure Shines is up and ready for school. Elaine continues her routine humming, *"Yes Lord"* and yawning becomes her backup singers. She sticks her head in the hallway and calls her daughter's name with authority. "Purpose!"
(As she makes her way to the back of the house to the kitchen still humming

*and she finds her daughter with her
head laying on the table).*

Child, are you asleep at the table?

"No!!!" *(Head still on the table.)*

No! Are you sick?

"No!" *(Saying it as though annoyed.)*

Who are you talking to child? If
you are not sick, you need to eat
and head to school.

"Maybe I am tired of school, I
could just quit."

You will do no such thing.

"You quit so, what's the point! I
can get a job. It's my life!" *(Huffing)*

Purpose baby, your education is more important than you will ever know. What's happening at school that has you upset like this?

"NOTHING!" *(Full of anger.)*

The devil is trying to discourage you because he sees your potential for greatness. He never attacks were there is no purpose.

"Devil the devil always the devil! I don't want to hear that right now. Like you said, I have to go!"

(Purpose grabs her backpack and exits the back door almost running into her Aunt Lucy.)

Woe! Slow down!

"Sorry, Aunt Lucy!"

(Aunt Lucy holds the door for a second looking at Purpose walk away and the devil exits through as well looking in Elaine Grace direction snickering.)

"Morning Lucy"

Morning girl, that daughter of yours almost took me out!

"She's going through something, and she is shutting me out. It's like overnight, she just changed. She is even talking about quitting school."

Not Purpose!

"Yes, and she made a point of
bringing up that I dropped out of
school at her age."

Does she not understand that was
a great sacrifice! You had to
overcome a lot to be here today. So,
give her to God.

"I know but she doesn't
understand right now her eyes are
focused on whatever the situation
maybe."

She will come around *(looks at the
clock)* Got to go running late. I will
call and check on you all this
evening.

"Ok, I got to get to work myself."
Elaine takes a moment and pauses to pray. "Father, it's me again, remember me, and remember Purpose."

Classroom

Just another busy congested morning in the hallways of Osier Elizabeth High. Purpose makes her way to class seemingly unaware of things transpiring around her. As she gets close to her class, she is approached by Ann.

What's up Shines thought you were going to call me back last night.

"I didn't feel like talking, sorry."

Girl what's up you know you can talk to me about anything. Have you told your mom about Dottie and her crew? Maybe she can talk to her folks or the principal. "What's the point, it will just make it worse."

Girl, I understand.

Dottie walks up behind them and knocks Purpose backpack off her shoulder. Oh, did I do that? I am almost sorry or maybe you need to learn to stay out of the way.

Ann speaks up, "Dottie you need to stop." *Dottie walks up close to Ann as Purpose picks up her backpack.* Now who are you talking to Ann?

Ann says nothing. That's what I thought! See you in class losers. Purpose looks at Ann and says, "Like I said, Like I said."

As the girls proceed to enter class, an unfamiliar man joins them. He heads straight to the teacher's desk and begins to unload his briefcase.

"Who in the world is that?" Ann said to Purpose.

Purpose responded, "Who knows and who cares."

Alright class everyone in your seat please. My name is Mr. Peters, I will be your teacher today.

(Purpose leans over to Ann and whispers) Oh, great a substitute.

Dottie raised her hand and asked, "Where's Ms. Brown?"

She will be back tomorrow.

Ok class we will start with the morning roll. When I call your name say, "here."

(Dottie looks back at Purpose and whispers.) "This is going to be to funny."

Mr. Peters proceeds to call names.

"Dottie Spring" (here)

"Ann Taylor" (here)

"Purpose Shines Jones"

"Purpose Shines Jones"

(The class begins to laugh.)

Dottie full of laughter instigates the situation and says, "Raise your hand shine."

My name is Shines (SHA-NECE)! Before anyone in the class knew it Purpose hit Dottie dead in the smacker. "What if somebody called you Dootie? What you have to say about that Dootie?" *The entire class suddenly got quiet.*

Ann quickly grabbed Purpose and sat her back in her seat.

That is enough, Ms. Jones, you will report to detention after class and wait for your parents. We will not tolerate this type of behavior.

"But she started it!"

(Slumped in her seat looking at Ann)

"See it doesn't matter."

Grace

Often what cannot be seen with the natural eye is one of the greatest assets of a believer. We face so many different obstacles often and seemingly alone but often grace is standing guard. That even when we face defeat, we are still winning even when the finish line is so far off. This is no different in the life of Purpose. Sometimes we must take a glance behind the curtain to understand.

2 Corinthians 12:8-10
(New Living Translation)

*Three different times I begged the Lord
to take it away. Each time he
said, "My grace is all you need. My
power works best in weakness." So
now I am glad to boast about my
weaknesses, so that the power of Christ
can work through me. That's why I
take pleasure in my weaknesses, and in
the insults, hardships, persecutions,
and troubles that I suffer for Christ.
For when I am weak, then I am strong.*

Heavenly Seat

The devil enters within heaven's jurisdiction and takes a seat where he can watch his tactics develop in the distance.

"Yes, this spot works just fine. I can see nicely from here." He then begins to laugh eerily as he ponders his next move.

God enters the room and notices the enemy sitting. "How dare you enter! What can you say for yourself Lucifer?"

Lucifer responds, "No need to worry, I just wanted to check out the view from the best seat in the house.

You need to depart with your foolishness!

"Believe me I have better things to do. You know I have unfinished business." *(The devil leaves eerily laughing.)*

God takes a seat and knows what he must do to deflect the tactics of the enemy. He knows the enemy will never forfeit his agenda willingly.

God speaks, "Jacob come forth!"

The angel Jacob appears and kneels before his creator.

"Yes Almighty."

Jacob, I have an assignment for you. I need you to go to a young girl, a precious gift named Purpose. She has yet to recognize the value I have placed within her for what is before her. She needs your guidance and beware! Lucifer is on the prowl. For he has unfinished business as well.

"I will as you have instructed."

Jacob immediately leaves the

presence of God and locate

Purpose.

Detention

Ann runs up to Purpose who is posted at her locker. Shines you got me worried girl. You know you can talk to me about anything. I'm here for you, I got you.

"I know girl, I just can't explain it. It's like I can't even recognize what is happening. It doesn't make sense to me."

"Ms. Jones don't forget detention starts shortly." Mr. Peters says in passing and walking right behind him is Dottie and she flips Purpose the bird.

Purpose launches at her and Ann grabs her in the nick of time. Mr. Peters stops, looks in their direction and taps the face of his wristwatch.

(Dottie continues walking and snickering with her friends.) "Have a great evening Mr. Peters."
You as well Ms. Spring.
Purpose slams her locker.
"You see what I mean it doesn't even matter, no matter what we do they always get away with it!"
It won't always be like this. Shines make sure you call me when you

get home, ok, ok? (*Silence lingers that had never lingered between the two friends and Purpose begins to walk away ignoring the concern of her best friend.*)

Ann says it once again, "Ok!" but she stands there with her own voice and the silence of her friend that she has never seen before. As she begins to walk down the corridor, she feels something brush against her creepily and she finds herself turning back in the direction her friend was walking and she whispered, "Lord, remember my friend."

Purpose arrives to detention and takes the first seat next to the window. She is glad in a sense that she is the only one sentenced to detention today. She slams her backpack on the desk and sits slumped in the chair. Unbeknownst to her she is not the only one who has entered the room. Lucifer sits upon the desk directly behind Purpose so he can continue to orchestrate his plan. Huffing and puffing Purpose says within herself, "I'm tired of this mess."

Some of the most lethal voices we can hear in our most vulnerable moments are whispers. *(Whisper) Yes you are, and nothing is going right.*

Purpose says, "Nothing is going right!"

(Whisper) You feel like giving up, and you're tired of living no one understands.

Purpose repeats, "I'm tired of living no one understands."

Mr. Peters enters the room. In Purpose's state of mind all she sees is disgust on the face of the teacher that *the whispers* have pointed out. Ms. Jones, your mother will be here soon and walks out of the room. As Mr. Peters exits the room, Jacob appears in the threshold of the door but Mr. Peters doesn't even notice him standing there. Jacob enters the room and immediately takes the seat next to Purpose and looks at Lucifer directly in the face and says, "You are dismissed!"

He looks at Jacob and tells him, "I will be back and I'm just getting started." He then exits the room leaving Jacob and Purpose alone.

Purpose sits with her head down on the desk unaware that she is in the midst of a war zone, a fight for her destiny.

Jacob speaks, "Hello Purpose."

She raises her head from the desk, it seemingly takes her a moment to focus on where the voice is coming from. Hello, do I know you?

"No, I am an Angel sent by God." Yeah Right!

"I am that I am," Jacob replies.

PROVE IT!

"How would I know you are thinking about disposing of one of the most precious gifts you have ever received if my Creator has not given me the knowledge to know."

WHAT GIFT?

Jacob replies, "Life!"

God? Really! He doesn't care anything about me, so you are wasting your time!

"He cares for you very much so. The enemy is out to destroy you.

He never attacks were there is no purpose."

My mom always says that. I guess you're one of them whitewashed believers.

"I believe that you are a survivor and God will make you an overcomer, but you will have to fight."

Fight, fight! What do you think I have been doing? Even the greatest fighter knows when to throw in the towel!

"That is why I am here; God has allowed me to catch the towel and I am here to give you the strength you need to endure."

Mr. Peters walks in the room and looks at Purpose strangely. "Ms. Jones who are you talking to in here?" Purpose looks at Jacob and he just smiles at her, and as she sits in disbelief and amazement, she never responds to Mr. Peter's question, so he just leaves the room.

Is this really happening to me? Are you really an angel? I know Pastor said we can entertain

angels unaware, but I never
thought it would happen to me.
"Many have been praying for you
because they see what you cannot.
Sometimes we get caught in the
cycles of life and forget the
promises God has given."
Promises?
"Yes, he will never forsake us but
more so he will never leave you.
He has been with you the whole
time. Placing grace in the moments
when you felt most defeated."
Grace?

"Yes, this is simply a moment in grace that required a special delivery."

(Tears begin to trinkle down her face)

God loves me enough to fight for me even when I did not want to fight for myself.

(Purpose's mother enters the room.)

Purpose what is going on?

Jacob stands up from the desk and says, "Hello Elaine Grace."

Hello Jacob.

"Mama you can see the angel!"

Yes, I do. When I was your age, he brought a word to me that saved my life. I had found out that I was pregnant, and I felt dirty, ashamed, and unloved. Before I knew it *the whispers* had me suicidal but God! Jacob said these words to me *(they both say it at the same time)* "The enemy never attacks where there is no purpose." And that is the reason I named you Purpose Shines. Because God loved me enough to allow me to birth a light into this world that will bring change that will give God all the glory.

"Mama, I am so sorry, we have a lot to talk about."

Mr. Peters comes to the door.

"Ms. Jones your time is up you may leave."

Ok, Mr. Peters and I would like to apologize for my behavior on today."

"It's ok Ms. Jones just never give up no matter what you face ok?"

I won't Mr. Peters, God's grace will see me through.

With a smile on his face. "Yes, it will, Shines."

Mr. Peters, you can call me
Purpose. Because I have come to
learn that God loves me on
purpose.

"Yes, he does baby lets go home."
Okay, Mama.

As they leave the classroom
Purpose looks back to see if Jacob
was still present, but he was not.
She was not dismayed because she
knew within her heart, she would
never be alone. Because she not
only knew but she believed that
God loved her on purpose.